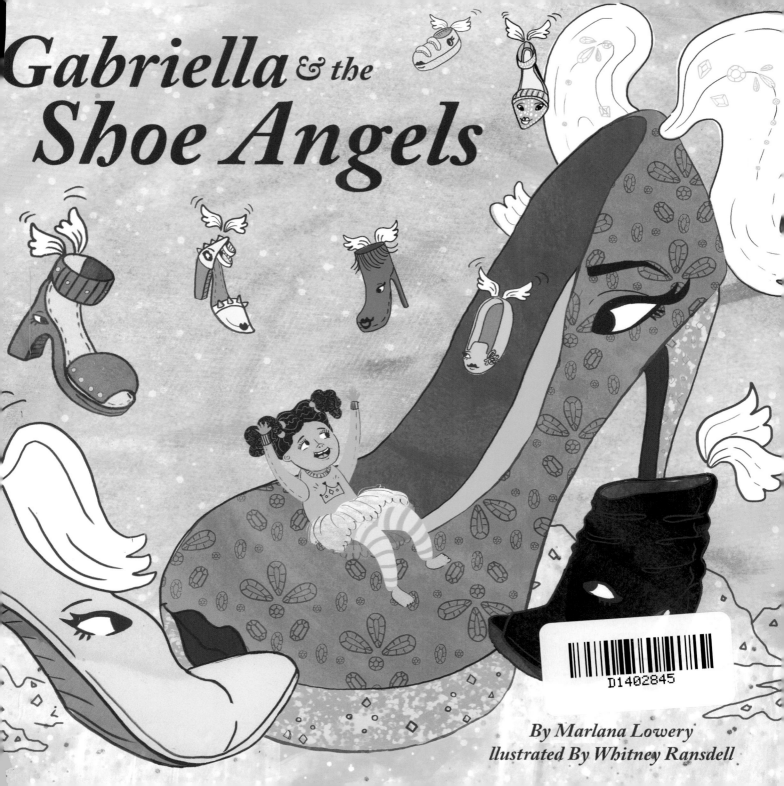

Gabriella & the Shoe Angels

By Marlana Lowery
Illustrated By Whitney Ransdell

Gabriella & the Shoe Angels
All Rights Reserved.
Copyright © 2016 Marlana Lowery
v1.0

Cover and interior illustrations by Whitney Ransdell. All rights reserved - used with permission.

Outskirts Press, Inc.
http://www.outskirtspress.com

ISBN: 978-1-4787-6903-3

Outskirts Press and the "OP" logo are trademarks belonging to Outskirts Press, Inc.

PRINTED IN THE UNITED STATES OF AMERICA

This Book Belongs to:

_____

Preface

For all the readers, educators, and shoe lovers from around the world, I hope that *Gabriella & the Shoe Angels* will inspire you to celebrate and promote the differences of those around you. We all are different, but we all have a significant purpose to fulfill.

May you read this book with an open mind and heart to receive the message of giving back to the community of those less fortunate. Also, from an educator's perspective, *Gabriella & the Shoe Angels* can promote literacy, colors, and measurements, in addition to diversity and etiquette. I hope you have fun reading and learning.

Sincerely,
Marlana Lowery

Acknowledgments

I am truly grateful for the creative mind that God has given me to write and tell stories that will inspire a generation to read and think outside of the box. I give a special thanks to my husband for his unwavering support and willingness to invest in my dreams. I give a big thanks to my children who motivate me daily by pushing me to become all that God created me to be. Thank you to my family and friends who have been there from the beginning with words of encouragement and insight along the way. Thank you, everyone, who donated shoes to make the shoe drive a huge success. To my illustrator Whitney, who was able to take this body of work and bring each shoe angel to life . . . You are a true gem.

One Sunday morning, the shoe angels were sent on assignment to visit a baby girl named Gabriella. Gabriella was only 11 months old when the shoe angels arrived in her bedroom. It was three o'clock in the morning, and the whole house was sound asleep until baby Gabriella was awakened by shoe angels flying around in a circle over her crib trying to get her attention.

The yellow stiletto was the loudest of them all, singing, "Gabby, Gabby, you won't fall, step inside and you'll be tall. You will shine like the sun when you're with me, giving you energy and lots of glee. You will have an everlasting glow that shimmers from your head to your toes."

Then the little pink flat with a hint of bling started singing, "Pretty as can be, I may be flat, but I'm fancy and free. Choose me, choose me! I'm soft and light. I'm the one all little girls like. I represent the little princesses all across the globe. I rule the wardrobe of every little girl I know. You and I together will do great things as we walk and bring pink on the scene. We'll leave sparkles everywhere, and the little girls will know the pink shoe angel was there."

Gabriella lay in her crib smiling and laughing as the shoe angels sang to her, but when the pink and bling flat dropped sparkles on her face, Gabriella became very excited, kicking her legs. She was so loud with laughter that she woke her mother from out of her sleep.

Gabriella's mother rushed to her room to see what was going on because she thought Gabriella's brothers were trying to wake her up like they always do. To her surprise, Gabriella was alone in her crib with a smile on her face. Gabriella's mother closed the door and went back to bed. The shoe angels started circling the crib again.

The purple shoe said, "That was close. We're going to have to quiet it down, ladies, before we wake up the whole family."

The yellow stiletto shouted, "Pink, you're dropping sparkles all over her face causing too much excitement! Did you forget that we're supposed to be a secret?"

The shiny black heel barged in and said, "That's why *I'm* here. I don't make a lot of noise. I just stand tall and poised. I'm classy, I'm chic; I bring all colors to their feet. My presence is so strong when you're with me you can never go wrong. I can be a pump, I can be a flat, I can be the stiletto heel that goes tap, tap, tap. I'll never go out of style. I'm so amazing that I make the world go *Wow!* Pair me with the little black dress. *I'm* who you need when you want to look your best."

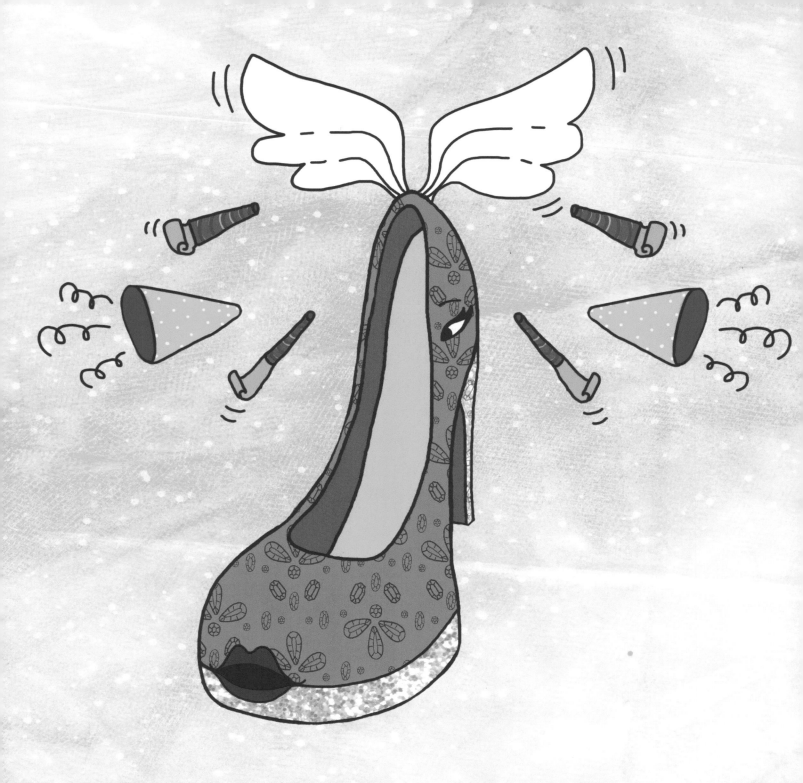

The sparkling red stiletto laughed and said, "*Ha!* You all think that you're so bright, but I'm the one that brings this party to life. Gabby, darling, I'll command all the attention you will ever need. Though I look like a tantrum, my manners scream, *Please!* I'm the siren that commands the cars off the street. I'm fabulous all by myself, but when the others need a boost, I'll give them some help. Some may think that I'm too loud, but I'm just a natural for drawing crowds. My name is Red, and when you walk with me, you'll have confidence and style."

The blue-fringed stiletto boots said, "Yes, you're loud, but it's *me* that brings class and style. I'm royal and rich, and I make the world smile. Some may cringe when they see my fringe, but there's no denying I've started a trend. I'm fashionably smart with a soft, kind heart. I'm on my mark, jet, set, and go! Gabby, I'll teach you everything you need to know. Allow me to bring out the fashionista in you, as we walk in style and be blue, blue, blue."

The blue stiletto came closer to her face, tickling Gabriella with the fringes, and she became so ruffled with excitement and laughter that she pulled a fringe off the blue boot.

"Oh no! Not my fringe!" cried the blue stiletto boot.

"You should not have gotten so close in her face, Blue. What in the world were you thinking?" said the neutral heel.

Blue replied, "She's just a baby. I didn't expect her to yank off my fringe. She's pretty strong!"

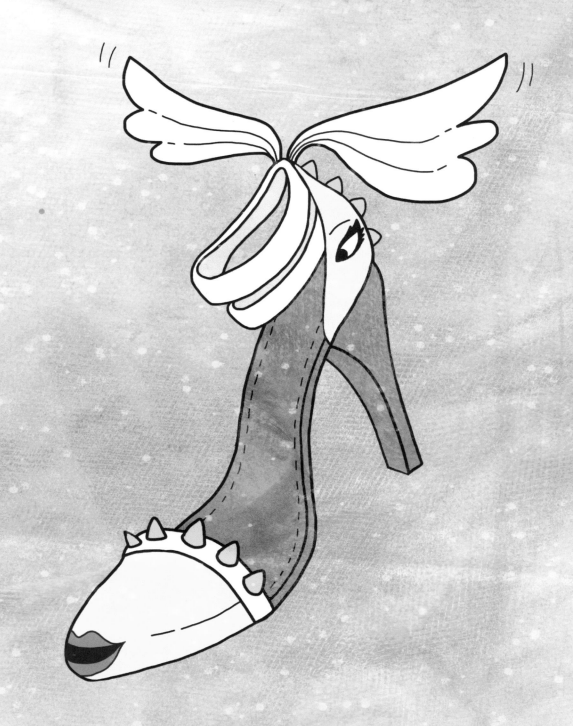

The neutral heel with the golden spikes said, "Oh . . . whatever, who cares? Gabriella will see that *I'm* the one who is fair. I make things blend, never taking over, just being a good friend. It's me, it's me who will make things right. Gabriella, we won't ever have a fight. I'm your go-to girl because all the others try to rule the foot world. I will take your lead and go with the flow, still being neutral yet rocking the show."

The golden sneaker said, "Now that *I'm* here, you all can disappear. Gabriella, they are the ones your feet should fear. I provide comfort, safety, and speed. I'm the only shoe you will ever need. You will walk, you will run, you will be the fastest and have all the fun. You will be crowned with trophies, medals, and money because your feet will be gifted and sweet as honey. I may not be tall, but I have a grip that won't let you fall. I'll protect you when the others are trying to be cute, but with me, your feet will never have a dispute. I have a sparkle, I have a shine; my value goes deep as an African gold mine."

Purple said, "Medals and money, really? Oh, what a spiel, but too bad you're not as glamorous as these heels. Gabby, once you step inside these shoes, you will feel new, new, new. My color is bright and oh so rich. Once you start walking, you'll experience pure bliss. Check out the golden details with my tan leather trim. I'm so refined that I make you want to swim. I'm not too high, and definitely not short, but when they see you coming, you'll get a good report."

*L*astly, the sparkling pump with the golden bottom said, "Stop it, stop it, stop it now! There's enough of us to go around! Gabriella, we're not here to fight. We're here because you've been chosen to make the world bright. You're called to make it a better place by putting a smile on someone's face. No matter what the race or creed, you'll provide shoes for those in need. You will gather your family and friends once a year to celebrate you and spread shoe cheer.

"So, my fellow shoe angels, we don't have to compete, because we are all beautiful and unique. We share the same mission—for no person to be without shoes, to make them smile, and take away their blues. We make life a little more fun, providing feet protection as they walk or run. For every heel and every flat, your purpose is to support and to always have your owner's back. We all have a special flair that brings confidence for every woman and little girl to walk and swing their hair."

lack said, "Yes, you're right, Sparkle, there's no need for us to fight. We need to celebrate each other's differences and think about how we're going to change the lives of so many feet all across the globe! Come on, ladies, let's bring it in and hug real tight."

All of the shoe angels came in closer to do their group hug. Gabriella waved her hands at the shoe angels and smiled as they dropped glitter dust all throughout her crib.

Gabriella's mother came back into her room because she was unable to sleep from all the giggles she heard coming from Gabriella's room.

"Oh my! Gabby, where did all the sparkles come from?" asked her mother. Gabby lay in her bed laughing and cooing as her mother massaged her hands.

The End

CPSIA information can be obtained at www.ICGtesting.com
Printed in the USA
BVIW12n2241110316
439667BV00008B/76

* 9 7 8 1 4 7 8 7 6 9 0 3 3 *